FLYING FERGUS

The Cycle
Search and Rescue

KT-568-174

C016373388

First published in Great Britain in 2017 by
Piccadilly Press
80-81 Wimpole Street, London, W1G 9RE
www.piccadillypress.co.uk

A CIP catalogue record for this book is available from the British Library.

ISBN: 978-1-848-12620-6
also available as an ebook

Typeset in Berkeley Oldstyle
Printed and bound by Clays Ltd, St Ives PLC

Piccadilly Press is an imprint of Bonnier Zaffre,
a Bonnier Publishing Company
www.bonnierpublishingfiction.co.uk

FLYING FERGUS

The Cycle Search and Rescue

CHRIS HOY
with Joanna Nadin

Illustrations by Clare Elsom

Piccadilly
PRESS

Meet Fergus
and his friends...

Fergus

Chimp

Daisy

Grandpa Herc

Jambo Patterson

Mum

Calamity Coogan

Minnie McLeod

Choppy Wallace

Dermot Eggs

Mikey McLeod

Wesley Wallace

Belinda Bruce

To the Highlands
FIFTH BRIDGE
Evening News Offices
EVENING NEWS
PRINCESS STREET
To Portobello Bay
MIDDLEBANK
Home of Wallace's Winners

Meet Princess Lily
and her friends. . .

Hector Hamilton

Princess Lily

Unlucky Luke

Percy the Pretty Useless

Demelza

Douglas

Dimmock

Prince Waldorf

King Woebegot

Hounds of Horribleness

Queen Woebegot

Knights of No Nonsense

THE CASTLE

Turret of Terror

Stables

Entrance to dungeon

Cook's pantry

Hounds of Horribleness Kennels

THE TRAINING TRACK

THE ENCHANTED FOREST

Stuck on the Same Team

Fergus Hamilton was an ordinary nine-year-old boy. He liked dogs (especially his own mongrel Chimp, who spent most of his time digging for sausages), cats (except Mrs MacCafferty's cat Carol, who spent most of her time chasing Chimp), and ferrets (in particular Mr Miggins' ferret Kevin, who spent most of his time chasing Carol). He didn't like spiders (but he didn't scream when he saw one), cockroaches (but he'd never seen one), or sharks (but there weren't any in Portobello Bay, so he figured he was safe).

Yes, he was ordinary in almost every way, except one. Because, for a small boy, Fergus Hamilton had an extraordinarily big imagination.

Some days he imagined he could tame a wild bear and teach it to do tap dancing and knitting and long division.

Some days he imagined Chimp could talk all the time, and not just when Fergus back-pedalled into the parallel universe Nevermore, where his friends Princess Lily and Unlucky Luke lived (and where his dad Hector Hamilton had disappeared to when he was a baby, imprisoned by King Woebegot after a squabble over a cycle race).

And some days he imagined he lived in Nevermore too, in a castle turret, with a pet dragon, and a place in the new cycling squad his dad was going to set up (now that cycling had finally been un-banned by Lily's dad).

But this morning Fergus was thinking that, for once, he was really quite happy living above his Grandpa Herc's shop on Napier Street.

His mum had a brilliant boyfriend – Jambo Patterson, the sports reporter on the *Evening News*, and Grandpa's second-hand cycle business was going great guns, what with all the publicity when Fergus and the gang had won the National Championships.

Best of all, now the Nationals were over, the team could get back to how it should be: Fergus reunited with Daisy, Calamity and Minnie on Hercules' Hopefuls, and Wesley back with his horrible lot, Wallace's Winners. Fergus knew Grandpa had made the right decision to join the teams together so they didn't lose their place in the Nationals, but there was only so long Fergus could tolerate Wesley's sneering and sniping, and today, Fergus thought, was just about long enough.

"Thank goodness that's all over,"

Fergus said to Daisy. They were on their way straight from school to the track on Carnoustie Common for the first team meeting after the summer break.

"Too right," agreed Daisy. "Now we can really get down to business."

"What business?" asked Calamity, tripping over his shoelace as he tried to dismount.

"Calamity by name and by nature." Daisy helped him up to his feet. "The business of winning the Internationals. Or had you forgotten?"

"Och, aye!" yelped Calamity. "In Manchester, too. My Auntie Julie lives there and she's mad with excitement."

"So is Mum," admitted Fergus. "She can't shut up about it. Jambo's covering it for the paper so he'll get to come too."

"I wish my mum was excited," said Daisy. "She thinks I'm going to be kidnapped by aliens."

"In Manchester?" asked Minnie, skidding to a halt next to them.

"It might as well be Mars as far as Mum's concerned," Daisy sighed.

"That's enough chit-chat," Grandpa said as he arrived in a hurry from home, with Chimp bounding behind him. "We've work to do. But first, a minor detour."

"A detour?" asked Fergus. "We've not trained properly all holiday, we need to get some miles under our wheels."

"I couldn't agree more," said Grandpa. "But not here."

"Then where?" asked Daisy.

"Middlebank," Grandpa said.

"But that's . . ." began Daisy.

" . . . Choppy Wallace's track," finished Fergus.

"I know, I know," said Grandpa. "You'll understand when we get there. Now get a shimmy on, you lot, we don't want to be late."

"For what?" asked Fergus. "What's going on?"

"You'll see, sonny," said Grandpa. "You'll see." And before Fergus could get another word in he turned and hurried on down the hill towards the gleaming velodrome.

Maybe they were just borrowing the stadium for practice, Fergus thought to himself, as the team followed Grandpa Herc down the path to the Middlebank Arena. Maybe Choppy was feeling generous and was letting them get used to a hard surface. The cinder track on Carnoustie Common was a bit different to the one in Manchester, after all.

Or maybe . . . but there was no way Grandpa would do that. Not in a bazillion years. He'd promised everything would go back to normal.

"Afternoon." Choppy interrupted Fergus's horrible thought as he nodded them through the gates and into the arena. Fergus felt his stomach sink. This wasn't a good sign. Standing opposite them, with as big a scowl on his face as Fergus had right now, was Wesley Wallace, his arch-enemy.

"So are you going to tell us what's going on now, Dad?" demanded an impatient Wesley.

"Yes, tell us," repeated his sidekick, Dermot Eggs.

"For once, I agree with Dermot," Daisy said. "Tell us what's going on. Do you know, Fergus?"

"I have no idea," lied Fergus.

He did have an idea, a very big and very bad idea.

"If you all shushed then I'd be able to tell you," said Choppy. "Or do you want the honours, Herc?"

Herc? thought Fergus grimly. *Herc?* That was a sign. It wasn't like Choppy to use Grandpa's first name.

"Fair enough," said Grandpa. "Well, as you know, kids, the team that won the Nationals was a joint effort. And the thing is . . ."

Fergus braced himself.

". . . the International Cycling Board would like it to stay that way. Which means—"

"It means we're all stuck on the same team if we want to compete," interrupted Choppy.

"No!" shouted Wesley.

"What?"
cried Daisy.

"Huh?"
asked Mikey.

Fergus felt his heart sink. He knew it. His worst fear was being realised. "But you said," he protested. "You promised, Grandpa."

"I know, and I'm sorry," said Grandpa. "But we don't have a choice, so let's try not to think of it as 'stuck', shall we? Let's try to look on the bright side."

"What bright side?" demanded Fergus.

"Exactly," whined Wesley.

"Well, you're already agreeing on something," Choppy said. "That's a good start."

"That's not the point!" snapped Wesley. "There must be something you can do, Dad."

"Like what?" asked Choppy.

"Make them change their minds," said Wesley. "Obviously. Pay them if you have to."

Grandpa shook his head. "There are some things money can't buy, Wesley."

"Don't be ridiculous," Wesley replied. "Money can buy anything."

"Not this time," Choppy said sorrowfully. "I tried, son, believe me, I tried."

Daisy shrugged. "He's right," she said.

"If that's what the ICB says, then that's that. We're stuck on the same team. It happened once before in Australia, in the Queensland Quicktrail. I read about it. The Brisbane Beasts and the Kalamunda Kangas made a right fuss but in the end they had to stick together. Those are the rules."

"But that means some of us won't even get to race!" moaned Mikey. "I only spent the Nationals on the sidelines because of the chicken pox."

"It's so unfair," added his little sister Minnie, to cross nods from Calamity and Belinda.

"No, it's OK," said Daisy quickly. "We can train as a squad, so the line-up can change. It doesn't have to be the same four who won Nationals."

"So you're all in with a shout," added Grandpa, giving Daisy a nod of thanks. "As long as you train hard, and try your best for the team."

"For how long?" wailed Wesley.

"Until the Internationals are over," said Choppy. "So the quicker you get used to it the better."

"You might even like it," added Grandpa with a grin.

"I doubt it," said Wesley.

And not for the first time that day, Fergus found himself in agreement.

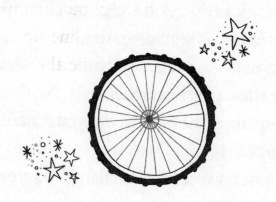

Out of the Comfort Zone

Wesley was right, Fergus *didn't* like it, and nor did anyone else.

"This is hopeless," Daisy moaned as Dermot bashed into her bike on purpose while she was doing a timed effort.

"You're telling me!" yelled Wesley, as he had to swerve to avoid Calamity, who was swerving to avoid Belinda Bruce, who had cut him up for the umpteenth time.

Fergus skidded to a stop at the dugout. "It's no use," he said to Grandpa. "We might as well give up now."

"What?" asked Grandpa. "And concede the Internationals without giving it a shot? Not on your nellie, sonny."

"Not a cat in hell's chance," agreed Choppy. "We're competing."

Fergus sighed. He wheeled back slowly towards the track, but as he stopped to adjust his helmet, he heard Jambo muttering to Choppy and Grandpa.

"They can't go on like this," Jambo said, as Minnie bunny-hopped right into the path of her big brother Mikey, who promptly flew over his own handlebars and landed on top of Calamity, who was already on the floor after a clash with Dermot. "If I reported this hoo-hah back to the *Evening News* then you'd lose any chance of support and sponsorship."

"You're not wrong," Choppy said.

"Aye," agreed Grandpa. "Something needs to change."

"But what?" demanded Choppy.

Jambo looked thoughtful. "Leave it to me," he said. "I might have the very thing."

"I hope it's to ban Wesley and Dermot," said Fergus to Chimp, who was quietly chewing a stick to see if it had any sausage qualities.

Chimp looked up, spat the stick out, and sighed heavily.

"No, I didn't think so either," said Fergus. "Worst luck."

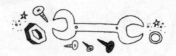

"The Highland Hundred?" asked Fergus, as the team settled into their seats in the kit room.

"It's a course that goes from the west coast up into the mountains," said Choppy.

"Beautiful little route," added Grandpa. "So I'm told, anyway."

"Little?" asked Daisy. "Isn't it called the Highland Hundred for a reason?"

"Well, obviously we won't do the whole hundred miles," admitted Grandpa.

"We might," said Choppy. "My lot can handle it."

"Okay, okay, we might," conceded Grandpa. "But the point is, however far we go, the distance will get you lot fit again, and staying away for the weekend will help you all bond."

Wesley looked at Fergus. Fergus looked at Wesley. Wesley stuck out his tongue.

Fergus huffed. "What if we don't want to bond?"

"Yes," said Belinda, nose in the air. "I've already got a bazillion friends. I don't need any more."

"Show-off," muttered Minnie.

"Jealous, sis?" demanded Mikey.

"As if!" interrupted Daisy.

Grandpa shook his head. "Kids, kids. You'll change your minds when you're there, I just know it. And if me and Choppy can get on, then I think you lot can too."

Choppy nodded. "True enough, Herc," he said. "True enough."

Fergus shrugged. Maybe Grandpa was right. He and Choppy had always hated each other in the past, and now they were getting on just fine. Well, better than they ever had before. "Where will we stay?" Fergus asked.

"I know just the place," said Grandpa. "Or rather Jambo does."

"Aye," agreed Jambo. "Hill House. Belongs to Mary Muldoon. She was an ace reporter on the *Evening News* in her time. Retired up there a few years ago and runs a hostel now for hikers and cyclists."

"Perfect." Choppy smiled. "Bags I get the main bedroom. And we'll all go up in the Wallace's Winners minibus."

"I can drive," offered Jambo. "Make it easier."

"You're not driving my van!" said Choppy. Then, remembering himself, "Just that, I'm used to it, and she can be tricky on tight corners."

Jambo caught Grandpa's eye and smiled. "Whatever you say, Choppy."

"Beast!" said Daisy.

Fergus felt his heart lift a little bit. Choppy really did seem to be making an effort. And he could see Daisy wriggling in her seat at the excitement of being away from home and all her mum's rules for a couple of nights. Perhaps this wasn't so bad after all. Perhaps this *was* what they all needed.

Maybe, just maybe, Daisy was right and it would actually be a little bit beast!

Over the Hills and Far Away

"Remember to brush your teeth," said Mum.

Fergus nodded for the tenth time as he zipped up his backpack.

"And call me when you get there."

"Muu-uum!" he protested.

"That was to Jambo," Mum said.

"I'll try," Jambo said, grinning. "There's no mobile signal up there, but I'm sure Mary will let me use the landline."

"She'd better!" said Mum.

Fergus felt his cheeks get hot as his Mum gave Jambo a quick kiss. He didn't mind her having a boyfriend, in fact he really liked Jambo. He just minded when they got all gooey in front of him.

"Och, I'll miss all my boys," Mum cried as she pulled Fergus and Grandpa into a hug. "You too, Chimp," she added as he barked a protest.

"It's for two nights, not two weeks!" Fergus pointed out, scooping Chimp up.

"Och, go on," said Mum. "Just make sure it's a weekend to remember, okay?"

The minibus pulled to a halt and Fergus peered out at the lonely stone house and the enormous trees that swooped and swayed in the wind around it. "I don't think we're on Napier Street any more, Chimp," he said.

"Are you sure this is it?" Wesley demanded, peering out.

"Sure as eggs is eggs," said Jambo.

"It looks a bit . . . basic," complained Choppy.

"If it's got a warm fire and hot tea and toast, we'll be grand," said Grandpa.

Fergus caught Wesley rolling his eyes, but he had to admit he was a little bit worried himself. It was the first time he'd been away from home and suddenly spending a whole weekend away from Mum felt a teensy bit scary.

At least he had Grandpa though, and Chimp and his friends.

And inside, it seemed Grandpa was right after all—there was a roaring log fire, and a table set with buttered crumpets, and best of all, Mary Muldoon herself, a tiny, smiling woman in an enormous pink cardigan, with hair to match.

"James Patterson!" she exclaimed. "Why, you've gone and grown up."

Fergus laughed. "James!" he exclaimed.

"It's Jambo now," Jambo admitted to Mary, giving her a hug. "But yes, Fergie. You didn't think I was born Jambo, did you? I earned that at school the year I refused to take my lucky Hearts football scarf off in case we lost a match."

"I knew that," said Fergus quickly.

"I wasn't born Calamity!" Calamity joined in.

"But I see you're living up to it now,"

Mary said as Calamity upended the crumpets onto the carpet, where Chimp snaffled them up before Fergus could say "lickety-split".

"Idiot," said Wesley.

"Yeah, idiot," said Dermot.

"Sorry," said Calamity, crestfallen.

"Not just you, that dog too!" complained Wesley. "I said we should never have brought it."

Fergus bristled as he remembered.

"Och, it's no matter," said Mary, giving Chimp's head a good scratch. "This little fellow is as welcome as you. Now why don't you check out your sleeping arrangements while I rustle up some more crumpets?"

"Good idea," said Grandpa. "Come on, gang."

"Gang?" huffed Choppy.

"Absolutely," said Jambo. "You're all in this together. Or had you forgotten?"

Choppy harrumphed but muttered "Yes, yes" before stomping off up the stairs, Wesley and Dermot in hot pursuit.

Fergus sidled up to Daisy as they followed Belinda and Mikey. "Want to share a room, Dais?" he asked. "You can have the top bunk."

"Beast!" she said. "I brought my torch so we can do Morse code in the night."

"And I've got all my Captain Gadget comics so we can read before lights out."

"This is going to be brilliotic, isn't it?" Daisy grinned.

Fergus nodded. "I reckon," he said. "If Wesley and Choppy chill out."

At that exact moment, they heard a roar of indignation from upstairs.

"Uh-oh," said Daisy.

"Is that . . .?" asked Fergus.

"Wesley!" they exclaimed together. But their cry was drowned out by another, even louder one.

"Choppy?" they yelled, and scrambled up the last of the stairs to see what was going on.

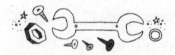

"Sharing?" exclaimed Choppy, staring in horror at four sets of bunks. "I have to . . . share?"

"Of course," said Mary. "Boys in this room and the girls next door."

"But–but–but–" blustered Wesley. "I've never shared anything. I want – no, I DEMAND my own room."

"Me too," said Choppy, still horrified.

Mary laughed. "You'll be sleeping in the outhouse, then. Did you think this was the Ritz?"

"Well, I think it's grand," said Grandpa. "We can have a midnight feast!"

Jambo swallowed down a laugh, and Fergus found himself grinning. He wasn't too keen on sharing with that lot either, but it was almost worth it for the look on Choppy's face.

"It's not funny!" said Choppy, his cheeks as red as radishes now.

"Oh, come on," said Grandpa. "Surely you can see the sense in this? We're here to muck in and rub along together. How can we do that if we spend half our time on our own?"

"It's true," said Daisy, glumly. "I read about it in *Cycle Monthly*. All the best teams bunk up together. Even Spokes Sullivan does it. But I wish all the Hopefuls could share together."

"At least Grandpa banned your mum from coming," said Fergus to his friend.

Daisy sighed. "That's true. She'd be in fits every five minutes about the germs I might catch."

"Excuse me," said Belinda. "I'm completely germ-free."

"Fun-free, more like," said Calamity.

"Well, you're brain-free," Belinda snapped back.

"Lawks!" interrupted Mary. "Listen to you all. What a lot of nonsense over nothing."

"Fine," said Choppy crossly. "We'll bunk up with . . . your *gang*, on one condition."

"What condition?" sighed Grandpa.

Choppy paused, and his grimace turned into a grin. "That we turn the Highland Hundred into a head-to-head between the old teams."

"What?" demanded Fergus.

"No way!" said Minnie.

"I'm up for it," said her big brother glowering down at her.

"Me too," said Wesley, eyeing Fergus.

"Me three," added Belinda, scowling at Daisy.

"Yeah, me three," sneered Dermot.

Fergus rolled his eyes. "Seriously?"

"Well?" asked Choppy, looking at Grandpa.

"It's too dangerous," Grandpa said at last. "You were supposed to be the chaperone, Choppy. You can't chaperone two teams at once, and I won't have my kids out on their own in the hills."

"So you come too," said Choppy. "Or are you too . . . old for that kind of thing?"

"Hey, hey, sonny," said Grandpa. "I'm not too old to get on a bike if I have to. But I'm old enough to know a thing or two about these hills and I know my knees aren't up to it. I'd hold them back."

"I'll do it," offered Jambo.

Fergus turned to his mum's boyfriend. "Er, can you even ride a bike?"

"Can I ride a bike? Born to the saddle me!" Jambo said cheerfully. "Well, maybe not born to it, but I'm not bad."

"Then it's on," said Choppy. "The Highland Head-to-Head it is. Now if you don't mind, I'm calling a team meeting. *My* team." And he ushered Grandpa, Jambo, Fergus and the gang out and shut the door.

Daisy shrugged her shoulders. "Back to business as usual then."

"So, if us girls are bunking together,"

began Minnie, "does that mean we can have a midnight feast too?"

"No," said Grandpa. "I was only joking. We'll all be tucked up and fast asleep by nine. No comics, no torches and *definitely* no midnight feasts."

They all looked disappointed. Team-bonding wasn't turning out to be much fun so far.

"Come on, kids," said Jambo. "Let's go see if Mary has those crumpets ready. I don't know about you but I'm going to need to get my energy up. Me. In a head-to-head. Wait till I tell your mum, Fergus!"

Yup, thought Fergus to himself as they trudged back downstairs, *this was going to be a weekend to remember, that was for sure.*

Pit Stop Peril

"We'll need to pack our waterproofs," said Minnie, checking her tyres.

"Definitely," said Fergus, as he clipped his helmet and checked it was tight. "And more food than we think."

"Spot on," said Grandpa. "I got Mary to make you a pack-up. Cheese sandwiches, fruit and flapjacks. If there's an accident, or a storm sets in, you don't want to be caught out without snacks and water."

"What kind of accident?" asked Jambo, looking a bit pale.

"A s-s-storm?" stammered Calamity.

"Och, don't worry," said Grandpa. "You'll be right as rain."

"Well, hopefully not rain," said Daisy. "I checked before we left and any bad weather is hours away. I've plotted the route as well." And she pulled out her map to show them. "See, it's along the flat at first, then a slow climb before we head up Henderson Hill and back down the other side to home."

"Safe and sound," added Grandpa.

"And miles behind us." Choppy appeared in the yard, followed by Wallace's Winners decked out in their competition strip.

Fergus couldn't believe his eyes. What on earth were they thinking wearing that? This wasn't Middlebank

38

velodrome, it wasn't even Carnoustie Common. This was the highlands!

"No jackets?" asked Grandpa. "It's awful chilly up in the hills."

"And have my team slowed down by all that flappy fabric?" sneered Choppy. "I don't think so."

"At least tell me you've packed lunch and snacks," said Grandpa.

"We've got biscuits and fizzy drinks," Wesley scoffed. "That's plenty."

"Fizzy drinks?" yelped Daisy. "You need water."

"And bananas!" added Calamity. "For energy."

"Oh, don't worry, we'll be having some of Mary's fruit cake . . . " said Choppy. " . . .when we get home an hour ahead of you lot!"

Fergus turned to Grandpa. "You can't let them go out without the right kit, Grandpa," he said.

"It's not down to 'Grandpa'," said Choppy. "I'm in charge – of Wallace's Winners anyway. If *you* want to be weighed down by coats and crumpets that's *your* problem. Now come on, team. Time to warm up."

"At least they're doing something right," said Daisy, as they watched Wesley and his lot wheel their Sullivan Swifts out to the starting point.

"For once I hope luck's on their side," said Grandpa.

Fergus couldn't believe what he was hearing. "I don't," he said.

"Nor me." Minnie backed him up. "They need to be taught a lesson."

Grandpa Herc turned to the pair. "Be careful what you wish for. A lesson out here can be pretty harsh. Your dad would tell you that." He nodded at Fergus.

Fergus gulped. "My dad?"

"Aye," said Grandpa. "This is where he used to come for training. And this is where he nearly came a cropper too. How do you think Henderson Hill got its nickname?"

Fergus felt a tingle down his spine at the thought of his dad being out here once upon a time. "What happened?" he asked.

"Did he fall off?" Calamity asked eagerly.

"Well, that's a story for another time," Grandpa said. "Maybe round the fire tonight. Now, it's time to get cracking."

"Yes, coach!" grinned Fergus, excited at the thought of getting some miles under his wheels and following in the tracks of his dad, too. Now that was something really special.

"You all understand the rules, don't you?" Grandpa asked the two teams as they lined up at the front of the house. "You'll follow the same forty-mile route and first team back to the house wins."

"That doesn't mean you can split up, though," added Jambo. "Teams need to stick together."

"Good luck!" cried Mary. "I'll be waiting with the kettle on, and cake a-baking!"

Chimp cocked an ear at the prospect of cake but he was too gloomy to wag his tail. Being left behind wasn't his idea of fun at all.

"Be good," Fergus told him.

"Och, he'll be just fine," said Mary, scooping Chimp up and squeezing him tight. "Won't you, my babby!"

Chimp didn't look like he thought so, but Fergus smiled. He'd missed Mum when he woke up in the dorm room, but then Calamity had started chatting and Mary had made him a marmalade sandwich just how he liked it – butter spread right to the sides, and the marmalade thick on top. Being away was different, but it was good too. "Come on, Hopefuls!" he shouted, joining the line up. "We've a head-to-head to win."

"Beast!" cried Daisy. "First place here we come!"

"I seriously doubt it," said Wesley, sneering over from the other side of the gatepost.

"Not if I have anything to do with it," added Choppy.

Grandpa rolled his eyes. "Just cycle hard and stay safe, all of you," he said. "Now, on your marks . . . get set . . . go!"

And with their heads down and pedals spinning the two teams sped off side by side – at least for now – towards the misty hills.

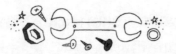

After three hours on the road, Fergus had to admit that his legs and lungs were aching, but his heart was pumping with happiness.

"Isn't it beautiful?" he yelled over his shoulder, as they pedalled past a vast loch and back into the trees that lined the winding road on either side.

"Brilliotic!" agreed Daisy.

"Amazing," chorused Minnie and Calamity.

"Jambo?" asked Fergus. "Isn't it great?"

"It's . . . it's . . . fabulous," Jambo finally managed from a little way behind, each breath wheezing and heavy.

Fergus thought of Mum, and how much she'd worry if she knew Jambo was struggling. "We should stop," suggested Fergus to Daisy. "It's nearly time for a lunch break anyway." And he signalled to the others to pull to the side of the road.

"What are you doing?" yelled Choppy, skidding to a halt with the rest of the Winners. "Why have you stopped?"

"Good thinking, Fergie," said Jambo, catching up at last. "I know everyone will be glad of a rest."

"Everyone?" scoffed Choppy. "You mean *you* can't take the pace."

"Now, now," said Jambo. "We all need to eat something anyway or we'll not have the energy for the climb up Henderson Hill."

"Eating's cheating," said Wesley.

"Agreed," said Choppy. "If we run out of energy we can drink on the way."

"You'll get stitches!" said Fergus.

"Or sick," said Daisy. "I read about it in –"

"Read about it?" Choppy snorted. "Listen, missy, I've been cycling more years than you've had hot dinners and I know *exactly* what I'm doing. So enjoy your little picnic, and we'll see you in a few hours. I'd say we'd save some cake for you back at Hill House, but we'll have worked up a nice appetite by the time you turn up."

Fergus didn't feel right about this at all. There was no way Grandpa would be happy with what was going on. "You can't!" he said.

"You can't stop us," said Belinda.

"So there," added Mikey.

Choppy nodded. "Remember what we talked about, Winners?"

It was Wesley's turn to nod. "See you later, suckers," he sneered at Fergus.

"Eat my dirt," added Belinda to Daisy.

And with that, Choppy's lot sped off leaving the Hercules' Hopefuls coughing in a cloud of dust.

"Jambo!" protested Fergus.

"Leave them." Jambo shook his head. "We shouldn't waste our energy chasing them. Choppy's an adult and he seems to know what he's doing."

Fergus sat down on the verge next to Daisy to eat his cheese sandwich. But as he looked up at the steep incline in front of them, and the clouds that were beginning to gather on the top of the mountain, he wasn't so sure Choppy knew what he doing at all.

You Take the High Road

Fergus pushed his sandwich wrapper inside his rucksack and stood up.

"Time to get cracking," he said. "They've already had a fifteen-minute headstart on us."

"Let's go!" agreed Minnie, jumping up and grabbing her bike.

"Might be worth pulling these on too," said Daisy, waving her waterproof.

"The rain's not due for hours," Calamity pointed out.

Fergus glanced at the glowering sky. "Tell that to the clouds," he said and pulled out his own jacket. "Jambo?"

Jambo creaked to his feet. "Ready!" he said and smiled. But Fergus could tell it was to cover a grimace. The morning cycle had taken its toll on Jambo's legs – he was more used to football than cycling, and Fergus wasn't at all sure Jambo would manage to get up and down the humungous Henderson Hill, especially in the rain.

"We can take it slowly," Fergus told him. "Better safe than sorry, that's what Grandpa Herc always says."

"Not on my account," said Jambo. "We're going to give it our all. 'Eyes on the prize' – isn't that what Herc says too?"

Fergus nodded. It certainly was. He took a last sip of water and stowed the bottle on its holder. Well, if it was "all" Jambo wanted, then he was jolly well going to give it.

"Let's go, Hopefuls!" Fergus cried. And together they sped down the hard tarmac towards the lilac heather and granite crags of Henderson Hill in the distance.

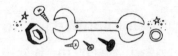

As the rain began to patter steadily on the plastic of his jacket, Fergus could feel his thigh muscles crying out in pain. "It's only lactic acid," he told himself as he blinked away the water and forced himself to push down on the pedals. "Just a normal physical reaction." He kept at it, his legs pumping like pistons. "Just a few more metres," he told himself. "Just ... a ... few ... more ... . Woo-hoo!"

He'd done it! He'd reached the summit. And oh, was it worth it! From the top of the hill Fergus could see for miles, maybe even as far as home. But one thing he couldn't make out was

Wesley's lot. He scanned the road ahead right up to the horizon, but they were nowhere to be seen.

Fergus turned to look back at his teammates. There was Daisy willing herself on. "One, two, one, two," she chanted.

Behind her, Minnie and Calamity were singing to keep their spirits up.

But, further behind them, Jambo was silent, red-faced and panting. Fergus knew what Mum would say, ever the nurse: "For goodness, sake, stop now before you fall over with exhaustion!"

But he knew what Grandpa would say too. "Just when you think you can't go any further, give it a little extra push," and, "If you're going to come second, do it in style." Most important of all, he'd remind them: "No rider left behind. Do it together, or not at all."

Well, Grandpa might not be here to encourage them, but Fergus Hamilton – number one rider on Hercules' Hopefuls, winner of the Nationals – was.

"Come on, Jambo!" he yelled. "You can do it! Not far to go!" He glanced back again to see Jambo grit his teeth against the wind and nod. He was going to do it! He was going to give it his all!

"That's it!" called Fergus. "Wallace's lot might have beaten us back, but we're still winners if we do this in good time."

"Woo-hoo!" yelled Daisy as she joined Fergus at the top. "Keep going, Jambo, you're doing great!"

"Amazing," added Minnie and Calamity who had made it too.

"Brilliotic!" yelled Daisy and Fergus together.

At that, Fergus could see Jambo giving it that last little push until he too joined the rest of the team on the brow of the hill.

"You did it!" said Fergus.

"WE did it," puffed Jambo. "Together."

"We did." Fergus nodded, remembering something else Grandpa had told him. Winning wasn't everything, and sticking together was a triumph in itself.

So, even though they knew they'd come second in the head-to-head, the Hercules' Hopefuls all smiled wider than the highlands in front of them as they wheeled over the top of the crag and down the rain-slick slope towards Hill House.

"We made it!" Daisy whooped as they pulled into the yard.

"Only just," Jambo managed, as he staggered off his bike, wheeled it into the outhouse, and then fell in a heap on the wet flagstones, tripping up Calamity, who promptly dropped on top of him.

Fergus propped his own bike against the outhouse wall. "Don't stop here," he said, pulling the pair of them to their feet. "Better get inside and warm."

"And face Wesley and the rest," Daisy grumbled.

"Mikey will never let me forget this," said Minnie. "But we might as well get it over with."

Thunder rumbled overhead. "The sooner the better," said Fergus. "Let's hope they've left us some cake."

The gang burst through the front door of Hill House to the sound of Chimp's delighted barking and the sight of Grandpa and Mary rushing from the parlour.

"Och, thank goodness you're back!" Grandpa cried. "We were so worried when the storm set in!"

Mary clutched a hand to her chest. "Chop, chop, inside all of you. It's braw out there." She peered over Fergus's head. "Where are the others?"

"Huh?" said Fergus.

"Choppy and his lot," Grandpa said. "Aren't they with you?"

"What!" Daisy exclaimed. "But we thought . . ."

" . . . they'd already got back," continued Calamity.

"So that would mean . . ." Jambo said.

" . . . that we won?" finished Minnie, with a grin.

The truth of it spread over Fergus like chocolate sauce on ice cream. "We won!" he yelled.

"We won!" repeated Daisy. "We won! We won! We won!" And the pair grabbed each other for a celebration hug as Calamity hoisted Minnie onto his shoulders and began to parade around the hall.

"Hang on," Jambo said. "Hang on just a wee moment."

Fergus looked up to see a frown on

61

Jambo's face, and it wasn't at Calamity knocking the lampshade with Minnie's head.

"They should have been back before us, Herc," Jambo said. "They left us behind at lunchtime."

Fergus turned to Grandpa and Mary, whose own faces were longer than a horse's. "Oh," he said, realisation sending a cold shiver down his spine. "If they're not back, then . . ."

"Where are they?" everyone said together.

"They must have gone off-road," Jambo said.

"Taken a short cut, I'll warrant." Grandpa shook his head.

"But where?" Fergus asked Mary.

"Och, don't look at me. I stick to the path and I tell all my guests the same." She turned to Grandpa. "Herc?"

But he only shrugged. "I've not ridden this route before. I've no better idea where you'd take a short cut here than in Kolkata."

Mary frowned. "We need to call Mountain Rescue."

Jambo grabbed the phone and held it to his ear. "There's no dial tone," he said.

"What?" Mary took the receiver and listened. "Och, no. The wind must've taken the phone lines down."

"Now what?" wailed Daisy.

"Stop that barking, boy!" said Grandpa to Chimp, who was jumping up and down frantically. "I can't hear myself think."

"Chimp!" said Fergus, crouching down. "Pack it in. This is important."

But Chimp wouldn't. He just carried on yapping and jumping . . . as if he was trying to tell Fergus something.

Then Fergus felt it: a sliver of hope sneaking in as he worked out what his dog was saying.

"Where do you think you're going?" Grandpa asked as Fergus headed for the front door.

"Er . . . Chimp needs a wee," he said. "Just going to take him out."

"Well, be quick," said Grandpa. "I don't want to lose you, too."

"I promise," said Fergus, slipping into the yard, closing the door behind him.

He was going to be as quick as the lightning that flashed overhead.

If his aching legs could manage it.

"That was genius, Chimp," Fergus hissed as the pair bounded outside.

"Ruff!" Chimp barked back in delight as he cocked his leg against a pillar.

"Hmm," said Fergus. "Well, maybe not genius, but thanks anyway." He peeled his bike away from the wall, flicked on the lights and climbed back on, not quite believing he was saddling up again already. But needs must.

They really must, he thought to himself. Mary and Grandpa might not know the short cuts in these hills, but he knew a man who did. Dad! Grandpa said he used to train up here. The only problem was, Dad was in Nevermore, and getting there meant getting the bike up to speed again, and sharpish. In the middle of a storm.

"I can do this," Fergus said to himself as he steered towards the safest looking bit of road, away from falling twigs. Chimp barked back. "All right, *we* can," he said, out loud this time. And with that, he set off, pushing down on the pedals as hard as he could, until, in spite of the wind and rain, and in spite of how tired he was, he felt as if he was flying. Then he let his feet back-pedal once, twice, three times . . .

All Change in Nevermore

. . . WHOMP!

"And about blooming time, too!" came a voice behind him.

Fergus braked hard and screeched round to see Princess Lily, hands on her hips, grinning widely at him from the side of the dragon paddock. Next to her stood Unlucky Luke, still with bear paws and chicken feet. Next to him stood Dad.

"Good to see you, sonny," he said.

"Though you look like you've been for a swim."

"Nice to see you, too!" Fergus smiled back, the worry about Wesley forgotten for a moment at the sight of his father's and friends' familiar faces. "And it's rain," he added. "That's Scotland for you."

"How tedious." Lily linked her arm through his. "Well, you're here now and you won't believe how much we've done already! We've all been practising

like billy-o. Waldorf's nearly beating me on the flat, and even Dimmock can do a wheelie without falling off. Well, sometimes anyway."

"I can go forwards!" Unlucky Luke piped up. "Most of the time." He looked down at his claws. "But it would be easier with trainers."

"And fingers, I reckon," Chimp piped up, finding his voice now he was in Nevermore. "Now you know how I feel." And he held up his paws in annoyance.

"Opposable thumbs," he muttered. "Imagine if dogs had those. We'd be rulers of the world by now."

Dad laughed. "Maybe that's why dogs *don't* have them." He turned to Fergus. "Lily's right, we've been going great guns but there's still a lot to do if we're to have our first race in two weeks' time."

"Two weeks?" Fergus exclaimed.

"Exactly!" Lily replied. "We need kit, we need to learn some tricks –"

"We need a track, more to the point," interrupted Dad. "And I know you've built one before, Fergus."

Fergus thought back to when he and Grandpa Herc and the gang had made the cinder track on Carnoustie Common. "Well, kind of," he said. "But I'm not sure it would be the same here. And where would you build it? That glade in the Enchanted Forest?" Fergus remembered his first ride in Nevermore with a shudder.

Dad shook his head. "No, although that's fine for a bit of a giggle."

"A giggle?" said Chimp. "With the serpents? The Swamp of Certain Death?"

"Okay, maybe not a giggle. The point is, it's not all about tricks. We need a track that will convince the King and Queen we're taking this seriously."

"No tricks?" demanded Luke. "So you're getting rid of our control panels?"

"No forcefields?" lamented Lily. "No flame-throwing?"

Dad rolled his eyes. "Och, you can keep those, but we need a new track, and that's that."

"So where?" asked Fergus.

"You're standing on it," said Dad.

Fergus looked down at the grass, and the piles of dragon poo all over it.

"Here?"

"Right here," replied Dad.

"Er, what are you going to do with those two?" Chimp nodded at the two fat, purple dragons happily having a fire-breathing competition at the far end of the field, scorching several trees and each other in the process.

"Douglas and Demelza?" asked Lily. "Oh, they've got to be moved to a cave in the Mountains of Menace anyway.

They're getting a bit big and my Dad decided they'd singed enough flowers and burnt enough furniture."

At the mention of mountains, Fergus remembered why he'd come. He had a team to rescue, even if it was Choppy and Wesley. They were all on the same side now, and they needed his help. And fast. "Can this . . . wait?" he asked. "Just that I need Dad's help, really. It's urgent and –"

"All in good time," Dad said quickly. "Remember, whatever was happening when you left, when you get back the clock won't have ticked on at all. You have, literally, all the time in the world."

Fergus let out a breath. That was true. He did have time to help both sets of friends.

Friends? Had he just called Wesley a friend? But Fergus didn't have long to contemplate that new and worrying thought, as Princess Lily yelled an ear-shattering, "Tally-ho!"

"What in the name of Waltzing Matilda was that for?" Chimp asked.

"Our first job," Lily answered.

"And what might that be?" Chimp demanded.

Lily grinned. "Rounding up the dragons."

"Put on your fireproof suits and helmets," Dad added.

"And your game face," said Unlucky Luke, frowning hard.

Chimp whimpered. Fergus gulped. This was not how he had imagined today going at all. But if he could brave Henderson Hill in a storm, then he could catch a pet dragon or two without getting burned.

Couldn't he?

Making Tracks

Fergus surveyed their handiwork. It had been hard work, but the dragons were happily in their new home and the track on their old paddock really did look magnificent. He and Dad had designed a doozie, and on Princess Lily's orders the Knights of No Nonsense had spent two whole days flattening bumps, building humps and laying the special surface.

"Looks dull as ditchwater to me,"

Waldorf whined. "Where are the snakes? Where's the swamp? Where's the *fun*?"

"Yeah, fun?" repeated Dimmock, his half-witted sidekick.

"I mean, all we have to do on that is . . . *pedal*," Waldorf spat.

"Fast," added Fergus. "You have to pedal fast."

"That's a skill in itself," added Dad. "That last corner before the final straight is a tight one, so you'd better hold onto your helmets."

"Besides," said Lily. "There's all the buttons on the bikes."

"And even I have to admit they're pretty cool," said Dad.

"Like invisibility," said Luke.

"And cover-up clouds," said Lily.

"And my hover knob," remembered Waldorf. "All my own invention, of course. No more getting stuck in a swamp for me."

"Not a bad idea," admitted Fergus, though he was sure the power of flight was cheating, really.

"And the special sausage dispenser," Chimp added.

"You just made that up," Fergus pointed out.

"A dog can dream, can't he?" Chimp sighed.

"There's still some danger, too," added Dad. "You never know when a slime spout might spurt up." Just then, as if to prove a point, a great torrent sprayed over the starting line, showering Unlucky Luke in green goop.

"Typical," he sighed.

"And no one can stop the Hounds of Horribleness running onto the track," Lily pointed out.

"Or the Monkeys of Madness," said Dad.

"Monkeys?" asked Fergus.

"Well, they *were* hulking great ravens," said Unlucky Luke. "Once upon a time."

"Until Pretty Useless Percy got hold of them and tried to turn them into palace parrots," snorted Waldorf. "Some magician your dad's turned out to be."

"Well the parrots were *your* dad's idea in the first place," retorted Luke.

"You mean my dad, *the King*?" demanded Waldorf, squaring up to Luke.

"Did someone mention my name?"

Fergus swung round to see King Woebegot climbing out of his motorised carriage, followed by the Queen, who was fanning her face and muttering wildly.

"She doesn't look too cheery," Fergus whispered to Chimp.

"When *does* she?" Chimp whispered back.

"It'll all end in tears," the Queen squawked at her husband. "Mark my words, Walter!"

"Well, if it does, then Hamilton knows what will happen to him," said a clearly weary King.

"Orf with his head!" yelled the Queen, triumphantly.

"Exactly, my little poison ivy," said the King. "Exactly."

Lily rolled her eyes at her mum.

Fergus gulped again and turned to Dad.

"It'll all be just fine," Dad said.

"Bonzer," agreed Chimp.

"Beast!" exclaimed Lily. "Honestly, Mum, wait until you see me speed round the slalom. I'm practically on my side!"

"That's what I'm worried about!" wailed the Queen. "Princesses should be upright at all times. Orf with his head! Right now. Before we even begin!"

Dad took a deep breath. "Why don't you just take a seat in the stand, and watch, your majesties," he suggested. "Fergus can give us a demo and prove that Princess Lily and Prince Waldorf will be safe as houses."

"Me?" said Fergus. "Don't you want to?"

"He may be pardoned, but he's still banned from cycling," the King pointed out. "For now."

"It's true," admitted Dad. He turned to the Queen. "So what about it?"

"Well, I suppose if the boy gets swallowed by a stinking sinkhole, then it's no skin off my nose," said the Queen, taking a seat.

"Er, stinking sinkhole?" Fergus hissed at Dad.

"Oh, there hasn't been one for at least five months," Lily said. "You'll be right as rain."

Fergus looked at the track again. The ground seemed still and sturdy enough. Aside from Dad, he was the most experienced cyclist here. And if Lily and the rest of them were going to get the chance to ride at all then he didn't have a choice anyway.

"You're on," he said. "Let's do this."

Princess Lily held the starting pistol above her head. "Ready?" she called. "Steady?"

Fergus nodded. He was ready as anything.

"GO!"

And with the crack of the gun, Fergus was off along the track, zooming down the straight and into the slalom, where he swerved left, then right, then left again to avoid the twirling posts made to look like unicorn horns.

"Nice work, Fergie!" Lily yelled.

"Champion!" Chimp agreed.

Fergus smiled to himself as he came round the bend on the back straight into the magic multicoloured moguls.

Up and down, up and down his bike went, Fergus steering expertly over the humps, which tried their best to throw him off by moving up and down themselves. *Beast!* he thought to himself. *This was easy-peasy.* And he settled back down into his saddle for the final straight.

And that's when it happened.

First there was a *creak*.

And then a *crack*.

And then the ground began to heave itself in two at the finish line in the distance – a giant chasm opening up across the track, and out of it rising a cloud of brown, noxious gas.

A stinking sinkhole! Fergus felt his heart drop along with his stomach.

"Flaming Nora!" Chimp cried.

"Watch yourself," yelled Unlucky Luke.

"Pull up!" yelled Lily. "Stop!"

But Fergus knew if he stopped, then racing would stop too. The Queen would never trust Lily or Waldorf on the track if he couldn't show that cycling was safe. No, he had to find a way around it. But it was huge.

Okay, then over it. Fergus scanned his handlebars for the speciality buttons.

Invisibility? No, that wouldn't work.

Smokescreen? Not right now, unless he wanted to disguise the disaster.

Bunny hops? They'd have to be bigger than any he'd ever seen done before. Not even Daisy's bunny-hop boost button would get him over this obstacle.

Then he had it! "The hover knob!" he declared. Waldorf's invention, it would give him ten seconds of hover-power. That should be enough to get him over any gap.

As he pedalled closer and closer to

the canyon, he poised his finger over the button. Any . . . second . . . NOW!

He pushed down and felt an air jet under the rear mudguard whoosh on. The bike took to the air. "Hold your breath and don't look down!" he said to himself. But as Fergus soared over the sinkhole, he couldn't stop himself, and looked down into the jaws of the smelly, grotty pit below.

"Oh, crikey!" he said out loud, and shut his eyes, which were watering from the stink.

Wham! Fergus opened them again with a start. He was back on safe ground and hurtling across the finish line, where Dad, Chimp, Lily, Luke and even Waldorf and Dimmock were all cheering him on.

"Beast!" Lily yelled as he pulled up.

"Bonzer!" agreed Chimp.

"Not bad. I suppose," Waldorf managed.

"Not bad?" Dad demanded. "I'd say that was a star performance, by Fergie *and* our track."

"And my hover knob," added Waldorf.

"That too," conceded Fergus.

"But the sinkhole!" protested the queen. "If that was Lily she could have been swallowed up whole! Orf with his head!"

"I doubt it," the king said. "Watch."

The crowd turned to see the sinkhole spew out a very dazed and dirty Dimmock who had fallen inside when no one was looking.

"They may stink," said the king, "but they're fairly sensible. They just spit out anything that doesn't belong to them."

"But now what?" asked Fergus. "The track's ruined!"

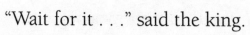

"Wait for it . . ." said the king.

"Wait for wh–?"

But before he could get the words out, the stinking sinkhole heaved a final smelly sigh and snapped itself shut again.

"Wow!" Fergus turned to Dad. "So does that mean we get the go-ahead?"

Dad turned to King Woebegot.

The king turned to the queen.

"Well . . ." she pondered. "As long as you all wear helmets. And knee-pads. And have the Knights of No Nonsense on standby for emergencies . . ."

Fergus held his breath.

"Then, I suppose . . ." the Queen continued, "it will have to be a . . . yes."

"Yes!" the crowd chorused, Lily and Luke dancing in a circle and Waldorf even managing to forget himself long enough to shake Dad's hand.

Waldorf could be nice when he put his mind to it, Fergus thought to himself, *a bit like . . .* Wesley! Fergus felt himself fizz with worry once again.

"Er, Dad?" he interrupted. "I don't mean to be a party pooper, but there is something else I need your help with."

"Of course!" Dad clapped a hand to

his forehead. "Go on, son. What is it?"

Fergus told Dad all about the head-to-head in the highlands, and what Choppy's lot had done, and about the storm.

"The eejits!" Dad said. "You should never off-road without a decent map, or GPS, and emergency supplies."

"I know that," insisted Fergus. "But they wouldn't listen. And the point is, where are they now?"

Dad thought for a moment, nodded as if agreeing with himself, then pulled out the track plan and a pencil from his kit bag. He turned the plan over and began to draw.

"Here," he said when he'd finished, handing it to Fergus. "This is what you need."

"What is it?" Fergus asked.

"It's the Henderson Hidey-Hole," said his dad. "Came a cropper on the mountain myself many years ago. If it wasn't for this wee sanctuary I'm not sure I'd be alive at all. I'd bet they're sheltering there like I did. Just follow the route I've marked – don't go off anywhere else."

"I will. Thanks, Dad," Fergus said. "It was . . . good to see you."

"You too." His dad smiled widely. "I do miss you."

Fergus thought about something. Something he knew he should tell his dad. "Mum's got a boyfriend," he blurted before he could stop himself. "He's called Jambo and he's dead nice."

"Jambo, is it?" Dad nodded, still smiling. "I'm glad. If it makes you and your mum happy, then it makes me happy too."

Fergus gave him a hug then. That way Dad couldn't see the tear of happiness that had appeared in his eye.

"Dead nice," echoed Chimp, as they climbed back on the bike for the ride home. "Nice enough to be, say, your stepdad?"

"Huh?" Fergus shook his head. "Don't be daft." He didn't have time for gooey stuff right now, he had five people to rescue.

And with Dad's map, he had the means to do it.

The Henderson Hidey-Hole

"Wesley?" came the yell. "Wesley, is that you?"

Fergus hurried from parking his bike in the outhouse to see Grandpa, Mary and Jambo in the porch of Hill House, hope written on their faces. "Just me," he said, and looked down at the soggy dog at his side. "And Chimp."

"Och, Fergie!" Grandpa took in the bedraggled pair. "We heard a kerfuffle and hoped it was the others."

Fergus shook his head. "Sorry. But . . . the thing is . . ." Fergus hesitated. How was he going to explain this? Well, he'd worry about that later. "I'm pretty sure I know where they are."

"Really?" Jambo frowned.

"Really?" Grandpa put his hands on Fergus's shoulders. "This is serious stuff. Not some imaginary game."

"I'm serious," Fergus insisted. "I–I worked it out. I've drawn a map. I remember a crag, and . . ."

Fergus had to convince Grandpa and the others, he just had to. "I promise," he said. "Cyclist's honour."

Grandpa and Jambo didn't need any more convincing than that.

"Can I come?" demanded Daisy, who was almost dancing on the doorstep in anticipation. "I've got a torch!"

Minnie and Calamity were looking

eager behind her.

Grandpa shook his head. "The rest of you stay warm and safe with Mary," he said. "Bad enough the rest of them out on a night like this – your mammies and daddies would be frantic if they thought I'd put you in danger."

Daisy's face fell. "Well, take this at least," she sighed, and offered her torch.

"Thanks, Dais," said Fergus gratefully.

"I'll drive," said Jambo.

"Choppy won't be happy," Grandpa pointed out.

"Choppy will be grateful you've found him," Mary pointed out. "He'd better be."

If we find him, thought Fergus, as he climbed into the minibus clutching the map and the torch. And as Mary slid the door closed with a clunk, he hoped harder than ever that Dad was right.

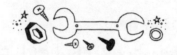

The minibus pulled up on a narrow track, its wheels churning into puddles of mud.

"Are you sure this is it?" Jambo peered past the windscreen wipers at a gloomy grey crag, slick with rain.

Fergus nodded. "Left at the crossroads, past the burned tree, and second crag on the right."

"This is the one," said Grandpa. "Come on. No time to lose or the van will be stuck in this mud. And then we'll all be stranded."

The trio clambered down from the van into the driving rain and wind.

"Oof," Fergus exclaimed as a great gust swept over him, taking Dad's map with it. "No!" he wailed. But the wind carried that away as well.

"We're here," cried Jambo. "No use for your map any more. If they're here they're here. If not . . ." Another gust whipped Jambo's words away.

"Brace yourself!" Grandpa yelled.

"I am!" Fergus replied, steadying himself and leaning forward into the gale. He surveyed the crag, looking for the entrance Dad had told him about.

It was hard to see in the storm, but with the help of Daisy's torch he could just make out an archway in the stone, and next to it, the unmistakeable gleam of a Sullivan Swift. "This is it!" he yelled, and scrambled over the stony ground towards it, the others following behind. "Wesley!" he called. "Wesley, are you there?"

There was no answer.

"Choppy!" Grandpa joined in as they squinted into the gloom. "Choppy, can you hear us?"

Still no answer. They looked at each other. "After three," Fergus said. "One, two, three . . . "

"CHOPPY!" they shouted together.

"Here," came a weak voice. "Over here."

"Wesley?" Fergus asked, trying to direct the beam. "Is that you?"

"It is," Wesley's pale face loomed in front of Fergus. "It's me."

"Thank goodness!" Fergus cried and, without thinking, threw his arms around his team-mate, who hugged him right back. "Are you okay?" he asked.

"Of course I am," Wesley said, remembering himself and stepping back quickly. "And so are the others." On cue, Mikey, Belinda and Dermot appeared next to him, all smiling in relief. "But my dad . . ."

Fergus, Grandpa and Jambo looked to the back of the cave where Choppy sat forlornly.

"I'm sorry," he said, shaking his head. "We got lost, and then–"

"No time for explanations now," Grandpa interrupted. "We need to get going. This weather's not going away any time soon, and night's coming in."

"He's right," Jambo agreed. "Come on, gang!"

"You too, Choppy," Grandpa said, holding his hand out to help his fellow coach up.

Fergus watched as Choppy took it and hauled himself to his feet. Then, shivering, Choppy followed his team out to the minibus.

"I've got the heaters on high," Jambo

said. He turned to Choppy. "You're okay with me driving?"

Choppy nodded gratefully. "Just be careful of reverse," he said. "It can stick."

"Right you are. It's pretty muddy. Fingers crossed everyone."

"Come on!" the gang yelled as the engine roared and the wheels strained to get a grip in the wet.

"You can do it!" Fergus cried.

And with that, and a colossal lurch, the minibus headed back down the narrow track towards safety, towards comfort, towards . . .

"Cake!" yelled Wesley, falling on to a fat slice of fruit loaf that sat on a platter in front of the roaring fire, Dermot, Belinda and Mikey right behind him.

"You're home!" Minnie cried, wrapping her arms around her brother.

"Hmmgghh," Mikey confirmed, showering her with crumbs, which Chimp promptly licked off.

"Gross!" said Daisy, but Fergus could tell she didn't really care. She was just relieved everyone was back safe and sound. They all were.

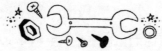

That evening, after hot baths and clean clothes, the whole team sat by the fire eating cheese on toast, and more cake, and singing folk songs with Mary. Jambo strummed a guitar, Choppy drummed on a biscuit tin and Grandpa played the spoons. Fergus smiled. Grandpa had been right after all, coming away was good for bonding. Eventually.

The song ended, and Choppy stood

up. "I've got something to say. An apology," he began.

"No need," Grandpa said.

But Choppy insisted. "Today was all my fault, I put my lot in danger, because I was so determined to win."

"That doesn't matter now," Grandpa said. "You're all fine. Thanks to our Fergus here."

"And The Henderson Hidey-Hole," Fergus added. "Cyclists have been using it for years."

"The Henderson Hidey-Hole?" Jambo repeated thoughtfully. "Where did you pluck that gem from?"

"Er, *Cycling Monthly* maybe?" suggested Fergus.

Grandpa raised an eyebrow at Fergus but he was smiling.

And so were Choppy and all the others.

"A toast!" cried Mary, holding up her cup of tea. "To Fergie!"

"To Fergie!" the others chorused, mugs of steaming hot chocolate clanking together.

Fergus felt his mouth smile so wide it almost hurt.

And to Dad, he said to himself. *Thanks for that*. And he raised his own mug high.

A Weekend to Remember

"Mum!" Fergus yelled, as he jumped off the minibus back at Middlebank stadium. "You won't believe what happened!"

"Och, Fergie!" Mum squeezed him so hard he almost came off his feet. "I've missed you. You can tell me all about it at home. Jambo!" she called over Fergus's shoulder, and he let go so she could hug Jambo, and Grandpa too.

He turned to watch the other mums

and dads greeting their kids before taking them home for tea.

All except Wesley, who was still sitting in the van waiting as Choppy unloaded the bikes. Wesley didn't have a mum, and Fergus knew how hard missing a parent could be.

"Wesley?" Fergus walked over to the other boy.

Wesley looked up. "See you soon," he said. "I suppose." And he sighed.

"I . . ." Fergus tried to find the words. "I was wondering if you wanted to come back for tea?"

"To yours?" Wesley asked, confused.

Fergus nodded. "It's nothing special. Just sandwiches, I expect. Or fishfingers. And the flat's tiny, and—"

"I'd love to!" Wesley interrupted. "Fishfingers are my favourite. Is that okay, Dad?" He turned to Choppy who nodded a yes at him, then another nod at Fergus, in thanks.

"Now that's something I never expected to see," said Grandpa to Mum and Jambo, as ahead of them the two boys wheeled their bikes side by side towards Napier Street. "Not sure it'll last, but I like it."

"Yes," said Jambo. "We really did have a weekend to remember, after all."

And it wasn't over yet.

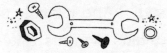

"I can't believe you went through all that!" wailed Mum as she plopped peas onto plates. "Why didn't you call me?"

"We couldn't," said Jambo. "Could we, Fergie?"

Fergus shook his head. "No signal," he said.

"And no landline," added Wesley. "The storm took down all the telegraph poles."

"And the outhouse roof!" added Grandpa. "We were lucky the bikes didn't get damaged. Poor Mary's got a bit of a fix-up job on her hands."

"Och!" Mum wailed again. "I can't bear it. My poor boys!"

"It was just a wee bit of rain," Jambo insisted.

"Rain or no rain, I missed you all," Mum insisted. "And it made me think."

"Think what?" Fergus asked, feeling suddenly a bit concerned.

"Well," Mum said, "it made me think that I don't like being away from any of you. And, well, I'd like that to be more . . . official."

"Official how?" asked Fergus.

Jambo looked at Mum. She smiled back at him. Then, Jambo put his hand on Fergus's shoulder. "What I *think* your Mum's trying to say . . ." he began.

"Is that I'd like Jambo to marry me," finished Mum. "If that's okay with you, Fergie?"

Fergus thought for a minute, Chimp's words echoing in his ears: *"Nice enough for a stepdad?"* He'd not pondered it properly then, but now, faced with it, it wasn't even a question. Of *course* Jambo was nice enough! Jambo was the best stepdad Fergus could possibly hope for. He knew how much Mum loved him and how much he loved him too, especially after this weekend. "Yes," he said. "Yes, please! Go on, ask him."

Mum turned to Jambo. "Jambo Patterson," she said. "I might not have planned this very well, and I don't have a ring, but I love you all the way to the highlands and back and, well . . . will you marry me?"

Jambo stood too. "Jeanie Hamilton," he said. "I would like nothing better in the whole world." And with that he gave her an enormous kiss.

"Ugggghhh!" groaned Wesley and Fergus together.

But it wasn't horrible, not really, Fergus thought. *None of this was.*

He and Wesley might go back to hating each other tomorrow. And the teams might go back to bickering. And Fergus didn't know what he was going to say to Dad next time he saw him.

But right now, Fergus decided, as he and Wesley and Grandpa raised a lemonade toast to the happy couple, this wasn't just a weekend to remember . . .

. . . it was one of the best weekends ever.

Joanna Nadin is an award-winning author of more than seventy books for children, including the bestselling Rachel Riley diaries, the Penny Dreadful series, and *Joe All Alone*, which is now being adapted for TV. She studied drama and politics at university in Hull and London, and has worked as a lifeguard, a newsreader and even a special adviser to the Prime Minister. She now teaches writing and lives in Bath, where she rides her rickety bicycle, but she never, ever back-pedals...

www.joannanadin.com

Clare Elsom is an illustrator of lots of lovely children's books, including the Furry Friends series, the Spies in Disguise series, the Maisie Mae series, and many more. She studied Illustration at Falmouth  University (lots of drawing) and Children's Literature at Roehampton University (lots of writing). Clare lives in Devon, where she can be found doodling, tap dancing and drinking cinnamon lattes.

www.elsomillustration.co.uk

Sir Chris Hoy MBE, won his first Olympic gold medal in Athens 2004. Four years later in Beijing he became the first Briton since 1908 to win three gold medals in a single Olympic Games. In 2012, Chris won two gold medals at his home Olympics in London, becoming Britain's most successful Olympian with six gold medals and one silver. Sir Chris also won eleven World titles and two Commonwealth Games gold medals. In December 2008, Chris was voted BBC Sports Personality of the Year, and he received a Knighthood in the 2009 New Year Honours List. Sir Chris retired as a professional competitive cyclist in early 2013; he still rides almost daily. He lives in Manchester with his family.

www.chrishoy.com

The Wreck-It Race

Training for the Internationals is under way, and Choppy and Grandpa think bringing a new coach onto the squad will shake things up.

And shake things up she does, in more ways than one. Charlie Campbell has some interesting training methods, like practicing yoga and entering them in wacky charity races – and their bikes are banned!

Will they make it through the Wreck-It Run in one piece, or will the team crack up?

Catch up with Fergus and friends in their new adventure

COMING SOON